MOST PERFECT YOU

By Jazmyn Simon

Illustrations by
Tamisha Anthony

Random House
New York

Random House and the colophon are registered trademarks of
Penguin Random House LLC.

Visit us on the Web! rhcbooks.com

Educators and librarians, for a variety of teaching tools,
visit us at RHTeachersLibrarians.com

Library of Congress Cataloging-in-Publication Data
Names: Simon, Jazmyn, author. | Anthony, Tamisha, illustrator.
Title: Most perfect you / by Jazmyn Simon ; illustrated by Tamisha Anthony.
Description: First edition. | New York : Random House, [2022] | Summary:
A little girl learns to love each part of herself, from her spectacular
hair to her big heart.
Identifiers: LCCN 2021017030 (print) | LCCN 2021017031 (ebook) |
ISBN 978-0-593-42694-4 (hardcover) | ISBN 978-0-593-42695-1 (library binding) |
ISBN 978-0-593-42696-8 (epub)
Subjects: CYAC: Self-acceptance—Fiction. | Mothers and daughters—Fiction.
| African Americans—Fiction. | LCGFT: Picture books.
Classification: LCC PZ7.1.S557 Mo 2022 (print) | LCC PZ7.1.S557 (ebook) |
DDC [E]—dc23

The artist created the illustrations for this book digitally.
The text of this book is set in 15-point Garth Graphic.
Interior design by Nicole Gastonguay
MANUFACTURED IN CHINA
10 9 8 7 6 5 4 3 2 1
First Edition

To my daughter, Kennedy Irie, who always has been and always will be the Most Perfect You. Thank you for teaching me about life and love. To my son, Levi—you are my sunshine. To my husband, Dulé—I choose you always. I love you three endlessly. And to every reader, young and old—you too are the most perfect you. —J.S.

To my mom, Joyce Mills, my first and forever art teacher, who taught me to love myself both inside and out. —T.A.

Irie ran down the stairs wearing her winter hat, her hair covered by the pink wool. The warm July sun streamed through the windows of her house.

"Momma, would it be okay if I wore this hat today?"

"You certainly *could* wear that hat. But *why* do you want to wear it?"

Irie sat on the
bottom step and
stared at her shoes.

"Well . . . I hate my hair. It's too poofy. When other girls play, their hair swings from side to side. Or bounces up and down. My hair doesn't do that. I want pretty hair like everyone else."

"But, Irie, I didn't make you to be like everyone else. I made you to be *you*."

"When you were still in my belly,
I had a conversation with God and
shared everything I wanted in a child.

"I said that I wanted you to have my favorite color of skin. And then I was shown the most magnificent rainbow, made of all the shades of every person in the entire world.

"I looked at all the colors a person could be until I found my favorite: the color of your skin.

"I said that I wanted you to have spectacular hair.
And then I was shown all the hair in the entire world.

"I looked at all the hair a person could have until I found
my favorite: your hair.

"I said that I wanted you to have sparkling eyes. And then I was shown all the eyes in the entire world. I looked at each pair until I found my favorite: your eyes.

"I said that I wanted you to have a kissable nose.
And then I was shown all the noses in the entire world.

"I looked at all the different shapes and sizes of noses until I found my favorite: your nose.

"I said that I wanted you to have a joyous smile. And then I was shown all the smiles in the entire world. I looked at all of the bright smiles until I found my favorite: your smile.

"I said that I wanted you to have other unique qualities, too. And then I was shown all the freckles and dimples.

"I heard all the precious giggles and stutters.

I picked my

"I saw all the long legs and short legs. There were big feet and little feet.

favorite of each

"All those extra things that make people unique—
I picked my favorite of each.

"Finally, I said that I wanted you to have a big heart. But I
didn't need to see anything. I simply asked that you be kind—
kind to others and kind to yourself.

"When you were finally born, I looked at you and you were everything that I had asked for. And as you grew, you were not only the most perfect you, but you were kind, too.

"So I am sorry if you don't like your hair, Irie. Your hair, and all the parts that make you *you*, were specially chosen.

"You are all of my favorite things."

Irie ran to the nearest mirror, took off her hat, and stared at herself. She studied her reflection, taking in every inch until a smile stretched across her face.

"What do you see, Irie?" Momma asked.

"I see my smooth skin. I see my beautiful crown of hair. I see my bright eyes. I see my awesome nose. I see my happy smile. I see the most perfect me."